Reuben

Book 5

Copyright

CONTENTS

ACKNOWLEDGMENTS

Thank you to everybody in my life who has contributed in one way or another to the writing of this book. My husband, my children, my children-in-law, and my grandchildren. You all are my unconditional fans. My BETA reader and grammar guru who make me look gooder than I am. [Bad grammar intended.] My fellow author friends who chat with me daily to exchange ideas, encourage, maintain sanity, and keep me from being a total recluse/hermit.

Mostly I thank God for the talent he has given me. I hope to hear you say, "Well done, my good and faithful servant," when I cross the Jordan and run into your arms —Many, many years from now. :).

About the Series

Sons of Honor Series

Adam

Seth

Jonah

Jacob

Reuben

Benjamin

REUBEN

PROLOGUE

Lantern, Texas - July 1882

"The twins are getting married!" Momma announced suddenly. Reuben Featherstone nodded to himself. *Ah, this is why the entire family was invited for dinner: Jonah and Jacob's weddings needed to be planned out.* His four older brothers and their wives or girlfriends were here. Reuben and his baby brother, Benjamin, were the youngest of six. Only he and Ben were single at the table. The family was getting larger and dinner was a bedlam of chatter and silverware clinking on plates. Seth and Purity's baby slept through it all in a wooden cradle in the parlor. Mercy's daughters from her previous marriage were quietly whispering to one another at the opposite end of the table.

Momma glanced at Poppa Monty with a smile. "And they both want to be married before Jacob leaves for college!"

She cleared her throat, but it didn't get everyone's attention like she had hoped. She stood and cleared her throat harder. "Could you all listen to me, please."

Heads turned at her insistence. Gradually all who were present looked at her. She smiled. "I propose… a double wedding."

"A double wedding?" Jonah turned to his fiancée, Theodora.

Reuben watched her tilt her head and pucker her lips. Was she considering it?

Momma sat, smiling at her twin sons. "The two of you have been inseparable most of your lives."

Jacob looked at Jonah. There was that silent communication Reuben had seen between them since he could remember.

"Ladies," Momma went on speaking directly to her future daughters-in-law. "If you're having doubts, or you're thinking you don't want to share your special day, may I remind you that you are marrying twins and the likelihood of doing much separate from the other is slim."

"But, Momma," Reuben shrugged. "Jacob and Charley are going to Boston. Jonah and he *will* be separate for several years."

"True. But when he comes back, they'll still be twins. I doubt that bond will be broken just because they spent a few years apart."

Reuben nodded. *If* Jacob comes back to Lantern,

he thought.

Honor smiled hopeful. "Now, Monty and I understand if you just cannot abide by the idea of a double wedding. We will do what you want, but keep in mind we are not the Rockefellers and one double wedding could be just as memorable as two, and, trust me, you're just as married once Uncle Harrison pronounces you Man and Wife.

Jonah took Theodora's hand and whispered in her ear. Jacob and Charley stepped away from the table to speak in private, in the kitchen. Purity walked into the parlor to check on the baby. Reuben dished himself some more mashed potatoes and ladled gravy over them. He had polished them off by the time everybody had come back to the table. The proposal of a double wedding still hung in the air, but there was an amicable spirit among them. Jacob glanced at Jonah, again that silent communication, and then turned to Momma.

"We think it's a good idea." Jonah and Theodora nodded together.

"Why not?" Theodora added.

Jacob and Charley nodded. Their eyes bore sincerity in their agreement. Reuben smiled, knowing Momma would be very pleased that they had agreed.

"Wonderful!" Momma clapped her hands. "Reuben, Benjamin, do you plan to have a guest with you?"

Sadness washed over Reuben's heart. He wished he could bring the girl he had fallen in love with, but alas she was already spoken for. "Momma, we've talked about this. Karena's family doesn't… She won't be with me at the wedding. But please do invite the Khan family. Perhaps I will get an opportunity to speak with her, maybe even dance with her."

Momma nodded. "Of course, the Khans will receive an invitation." She turned to Benjamin. "How about you, Ben?"

He grinned sadly. "I'm not sure."

Momma nodded, thoughtful. "All right. That gives me an idea of what to expect. Now, eat up before your supper gets cold. We'll speak to Uncle Harrison and schedule the date; I'm thinking early August so Jacob and Charley can be on their way to Boston."

CHAPTER ONE

Lantern, Texas - Earlier that Spring 1882

Reuben Featherstone stepped outside of the blacksmith's shop for a breath of fresh air. With the fire and heated metals, the shop grew unbearably hot while he worked, even in the last remnants of winter. His boss, Patrick O'Brien, didn't even look up from his work as Reuben stepped away from his anvil. Reuben wiped his brow with the back of his hand and watched a coach roll into town.

When it stopped at the hotel, a dandy-dressed man stepped out and turned to assist what Reuben assumed to be his wife. She was wrapped in fur to protect her from the cold, but the material that protruded from the bottom didn't look like anything Reuben had seen before. Trimmed with gold thread, what she wore looked like several layers of sheer, silky red material. The couple was dark skinned with elegant, sharp features. The woman bore a red dot between her brow. Were they royalty from abroad? What would royals be doing in Lantern, Texas?

Reuben watched as they gathered on the boardwalk. A younger version of the woman poked her head out of the carriage, looked around, then stepped down. The man quickly put out his hand and assisted her to the ground. She looked to be Reuben's age and wore a modern styled dark blue traveling overcoat and gown. She appeared to be Americanized, yet exotic like the couple.

Reuben's heart slammed into his ribs. She was the most beautiful girl he had ever seen in his life.

Curiosity moved him down the boardwalk, closer to where they waited for their luggage to come off the coach. The driver climbed to the roof and took down three trunks and three carpet bags. He carried a trunk on his shoulder, like a sack of feed, a carpet bag in his free hand, until he had set them near the Lantern Hotel entrance.

Reuben approached the girl, but the fatherly man stepped between them.

"Welcome to Lantern, Texas." The father extended his hand as if to block Reuben from reaching the young lady, but then shook Reuben's hand as if that were his intension all along.

"Uh, I'm Reuben, Reuben Featherstone… I work for the blacksmith, down there." He gestured, lifting his chin toward the smithy shop. "If there's anything I can help wi—"

"Ah, thank you." The man interrupted. "I'm Darsheel Khan; my wife, Anushka." He glanced to where Reuben's eyes were focused. "And… this is our daughter, Karena. She's engaged to be married."

The girl gasped but remained silent.

"Oh!" Reuben tore his eyes off her, glanced inside the coach for anyone else to come out, her fiancé perhaps, and then met Khan's glare. "I see. I meant no offense."

"Yes, yes." Khan muttered.

Reuben nodded, taking hold of two trunks left at the entrance, and gestured for them to walk ahead of him into the hotel. "Please let me help you."

Mr. Khan glared at the coach driver who had climbed back into his seat and was ignoring his previous passengers. Khan tilted his head in acceptance of Reuben's help, took the third trunk, and guided his family into the hotel. Karena kept her gaze on Reuben and smiled, then dropped her eyes to the floor and walked behind her parents. Reuben walked two steps behind her, pulling the luggage. Mr. Khan went straight to the desk where Jeremy Doyle waited with a fancy quill pen to sign them in. His twelve-room hotel was seldom completely full so when someone arrived by coach, Doyle was thrilled to have them stay in his hotel.

Mr. Doyle knitted his brow, watching Reuben bring their trunks in behind them as if he were the doorman or a bellboy. He ripped his glare from Reuben to his guests. "Welcome to Lantern." He greeted them in his heavy brogue accent. "Where we offer good ol' Irish hospitality."

"Yes, yes, I am Darsheel Khan, my family and I would like two rooms, adjoined, if possible. We might stay a few weeks. If things work out for me here, that is." He never smiled but was polite.

Reuben and Karena continued to glance at each other. Reuben caught her eyes and smiled. She ducked her head, but he could see her smiling, too. For someone who was betrothed, she seemed mighty friendly. Suddenly he considered his state. He'd left the blacksmith's shop because he needed to cool down. Did he stink? She smelled like a flower, something sweet, like honeysuckle or lilac. He gently inhaled, taking in her aroma. When she dropped her gaze to the ground, he quickly lifted one arm and sniffed. He didn't smell too bad. He hoped his sweat wasn't offensive. It wasn't as if he knew he'd end up standing beside the most beautiful girl he'd ever seen or that he'd wish he was more appropriately cleaned and dressed to impress her.

She smiled at him again. Her father had said she was betrothed, but there was no ring on her hand. Unlike her mother, she did not have a red dot on her forehead. Could that be the public sign of marriage for the women? She appeared to welcome Reuben's flirtatious glances. Had she noticed he'd checked himself for odor. If she was offended, she didn't show it.

However, Reuben considered, perhaps she was not offended by Reuben's sweaty appearance and possible odor because she was in no way interested in him. Perhaps her smile and downcast glances were merely her way to being polite to a stranger, or servant. After all, he was carrying their luggage.

She did gasp when her father announced so quickly she was committed to another man. Was that a sign she wished to not make it known? No other man accompanied them here. If she truly was betrothed, where was he? Reuben had so many questions.

"Of course." Doyle continued welcoming them. "We have a suite on the top floor, two bedrooms and a common room, if you'd like, or I can put you in two rooms on the second that share a door between them."

Khan leaned back slightly, to look into Doyle's eyes. He seemed to be considering Doyle's offer. Then he leaned forward and spoke softly. "What would be your weekly rate?"

Doyle quietly told Khan the prices.

Khan nodded. "I believe we will be comfortable on the second floor." He turned back to his wife and daughter, realized Karena stood next to Reuben, and moved to scoop her into his arm to bring her alongside him at the desk.

Doyle smiled. "Excellent." He filled out the hotel ledger and turned it for Mr. Khan to sign. While Khan signed, Doyle pulled down two keys to the rooms and handed them to Mr. Khan then lifted his eyes to Mrs. Khan and their daughter. "I hope you will be comfortable for as long as you stay with us."

Mrs. Khan jerked a quick nod. Karena barely glanced up.

Reuben adjusted the trunks in his grip. "May I help with these, since I'm here anyway?"

Mr. Khan turned to Reuben. "Young man, I assume your generosity is because of my daughter's beauty, but I must remind you, she is engaged to be married."

"Yes sir, uh, no sir. I understand. I just thought since I was here and Mister Doyle would need help carrying your luggage upstairs, I'd give him a hand."

Doyle grinned as he came out from behind the large desk. "That's mighty kind of you, Reuben." He turned to his guests, "If you'll follow *us*, *we'll* take you to your rooms."

Reuben found every excuse he could to wander past the hotel. Luckily, Mrs. Doyle ran a restaurant next door in association with the hotel. In fact, the lobby and the wall between the hotel and the restaurant had been modified with two wide-framed openings where people could walk from one to the other without ever stepping onto the boardwalk.

Reuben ate breakfast, lunch, and dinner at the Doyle's restaurant, even though it cost him a lot of his earnings from Mr. O'Brien's blacksmith apprenticeship, for the occasional chance to see Karena Khan. He soon learned the Khans' routine and knew when to gear his eating habits to when they would be in the restaurant. Her exotic beauty overwhelmed his heart and although he could not speak with her, he felt his heart sinking deeper and deeper in love with her with each passing day. The memory of the flower fragrance that surrounded her remained with him, and he sought that same flower in town. The lilac blossoms came the closest to being the same and had a nice bundle of blooms that varied from white to blue to purple. Hoping to have a chance to give her a fresh picking one day soon, he paid attention to where the lilacs grew. Never in his life had he noticed the locals' gardens with such interest.

On the rare occasion she walked through the lobby alone, he was able to approach her for a brief and superfluous conversation about the rain, sunshine, chill in the air, or warmer days. Anything he could muster to speak to her about he did. Until one day, he asked the burning question of his soul. "If I may be so forward as to ask you, where is this fiancé of yours?"

She smiled oddly. "I do not know. He and I have been betrothed since we were babies. By the time we left India, we were children. His family stayed in Vancouver, even though we were not readily welcomed as immigrants. Father continued to move Mum and me south until we found Lantern. I have no idea what his family did after we left Canada."

Ah, Reuben finally understood why her fiancé was missing. This betrothal was an arranged marriage. He'd heard about such things but had never known anyone who was actually committed to one. He wanted to know more about it. How solid was the commitment? Did he have a snowball's chance convincing Karena or her father to consider him instead of this mysterious childhood sweetheart?

Karena continued speaking. "People here are gracious. Father says he is able to work without prejudice for where we are from. And I know he wants to stay here."

She lifted dark chocolate eyes to meet his. It was all he could do to keep from taking her into his arms and kissing her soundly. He wanted to tell her he had no prejudice for where she was from, India, Timbuktu, or the moon— he did not care. She was the most beautiful woman he'd ever seen, and he wanted to spend the rest of his life loving and protecting her. But he could not do either.

"Father tells me when the time is right, he will write Thind's parents." She dropped her gaze coyly. Reuben crooked his index finger sideways under her chin and gently lifted her face.

"Thind? That's the name of your… fiancé?"

"Yes. Thind Singh. I have not seen him since Vancouver. I—" She turned away from him.

"What?" Reuben leaned in closer to her. The lilac aroma filled his senses. He wished he had picked some blossoms for her before coming here today, but he had no idea he would run into her. She shook her head and moved back from him. "I should go to my room."

"Is-is it not allowed for you to have… a, a friend?" Reuben gingerly held her arm, preventing her from walking away.

"Of course not. But a single woman should not be alone with a male person, especially when she is… promised to another."

"I was thinking about church or community events. Lantern has one church. The pastor is my great uncle. And there are a lot of social dinners and events. Could I escort you to any of these?"

"I-I don't know. It wouldn't be proper." Karena turned to face him. Her eyes penetrated his. He wanted to remain engulfed in her gaze forever.

"I would enjoy your company too much. Reuben, you make me feel—" She pulled out of his grasp. "I have to go."

"Karena, wait."

She stopped but didn't turn to face him.

He rushed up behind her and put his hands on her shoulders, leaned into her ear. "I think I love you." He breathed.

She shivered, closed her eyes, and pulled away. He watched her scurry up the stairs. He knew it was wrong to say it, but he *did* love her. If he was reading her correctly, she was interested in him also.

He had to find a way to make her his bride.

CHAPTER TWO

"Mr. Khan, welcome to Lantern's National Bank. How may I serve you today?" Niles Newbyer, President of the Bank, extended his hand to the new account holder.

Darsheel Khan shook the man's hand. "I wondered if I might have a word with you, sir."

"Of course. Come into my office." Mr. Newbyer led the way into the back. Dalton McVey and Jonah Featherstone smiled at them as Newbyer and Khan walked past the teller windows.

Khan sat in front of the man's desk. "People here in Lantern are very kind. I understand most of them are related to the Reverend, Harrison Lantern."

Newbyer laughed. "Yes. This is true about our little community, but thanks to newcomers like you and your family, we are growing and becoming more diverse. As it should be. So, I hope you are finding yourselves fitting in, settling down, and contemplating staying here a long time."

"Yes, yes." Khan cleared his throat. "Miss Mabel Bivens rented us a pleasant home on Third Street. It was good to move out of the hotel, although Mr. Doyle was very accommodating while we stayed there. However, it's good to have a place of our own." Mr. Khan cleared his throat again. "Mr. Newbyer, my family and I come from a province in India called Punjab. Due to a change in land reform laws and disenfranchisement of British rule, the economy became such that we were encouraged to go abroad to find work. And so, we did, but… securing work in North America has been… limited for foreigners. We could not settle where we first disembarked, uh, in Canada. Therefore, I moved my family farther south until we came here, to Lantern, Texas. I have been able to secure employment with your lumber yard, and we find this town to be… welcoming."

"Yes," Mr. Newbyer leaned back in his chair. "I must confess the town's grapevine is very efficient in communicating your procurement of employment with Bob Petre. It warms my heart to know you find our town to be a good place to settle. I'd like to think that is due mostly to our founders and their good Christian values."

Khan nodded. "In my frequent moves from far north to here, I have observed some things… in the economy, and I am troubled by what I see. If you would allow me to give you some advice based on my observations."

Newbyer nodded.

"I see a depression taking effect across this country, and I hope to help this community to avoid some serious downfalls."

Newbyer slowly leaned forward, steepled her fingers, and frowned. "You have my attention, Mr. Khan."

"And this… Mister Newbyer… listened to you?" Anushka poured her husband a cup of tea.

"Yes. He was very cordial and wanted to know what I thought."

"So, you told him about the signs of an economic contraction?"

"Yes." Khan sipped his tea smugly. "We discussed all that and I gave him suggestions to avoid it, at least how he could advise Lantern's residents who invest in the industries and such can avoid it. At the very least, they won't lose money on investments that have looked profitable in the past but will be ruinous in the near future: transportation systems, for example. I told him how we've seen this before and if they'll wait a few years before investing heavily, they will come out ahead."

Anushka nodded. "And he listened… to you?"

"Yes." Darsheel smiled. "He did more than listen, Anushka. He offered me a position with the bank."

"What? Oh, Darsheel! How wonderful. As what?"

"As a financial consultant. It's part-time for now, but if it pans out, it could be full-time, and I will receive a commission on the earnings."

Anushka sat still with a smile curled at the corners of her open mouth.

"For now, I will continue to work for Mister Petre at the lumberyard. He, too, appreciates my developing contracts for large lumber shipments with builders and architects as far away as Oklahoma. Plus, I will have set days and hours to give financial advice at the bank, possibly two days a week."

Anushka clasped her hands and bit her lip. "Oh, Darsheel. Thank God we didn't give up and go back to Punjab. Finally, we have found where we belong in America. Although I miss the Catholic Church, Lantern's Pastor Harrison is a good, god fearing man, and so kind."

"Yes. Mister Newbyer said he feels this town's

general atmosphere of goodness is due to its founders. Whatever it is, this is the first place we have come to that I honestly feel we can live and not be ridiculed for who we are and where we come from."

"Speaking of which." Anushka swallowed. "There's one more issue we need to discuss."

"What's that?"

"Our daughter's engagement."

"No!" Darsheel set his teacup down firmly. "You speak of breaking our vow to the Singh family?"

Anushka nodded. "We have heard nothing since Vancouver, darling. How do we know they wish to follow through? How do we know they did not go back to India?" She crossed herself. "Or that they are even still alive, God forbid." She drew in a deep breath. "How do we know they do not wish to break this vow with our daughter? Thind should have contacted her three years ago, when they reached marrying age."

"I am a man of my word! I will not break our vow! Now that we are finally settled and I have a respectable income, we will contact Bhagat Singh and let him know Karena and Thind can be married."

"But Darsheel…" Anushka sensed she was not

alone with her husband. She turned toward the parlor. Karena stood there, staring at her parents with tears pooling in her eyes. Anushka pursed her lips and lowered her head. She glanced at her daughter with sad eyes. Karena turned and ran to her bedroom. Anushka touched her husband's arm. "Darsheel, darling, everything has changed since we left India. Perhaps it is a valid thought that Thind no longer wishes to marry Karena. Our families are no longer—"

"I am a man of my word!" He slammed his fist on the table, making the china cups rattle in the saucers. Anushka jumped and lowered her eyes to her lap.

"I am sorry." Darsheel softened his tone. "All I have left is my integrity. Please do not ask me to give it up also."

Anushka lifted her eyes to her husband's. "You are an honorable man, and I love you."

"I love you, too, Anushka. I always have."

Anushka spoke softly. "Is it wrong to wish the same for your daughter?"

CHAPTER THREE

Karena threw herself on her bed. The tears she had been biting back fell, saturating her pillow cover. Anger roiled in her gut and she slammed her fist into the feathery mound. "This is so wrong!"

She sat up. A wave of warmth washed over her. The thought of Reuben's physique from swinging a blacksmith's hammer ignited a fire inside her. She longed to be held in his muscular arms and feel the firmness of his chest. She could see his muscles under his shirt bulging and stretching taut the material with each passing week. This occupation for which he apprenticed was building him into a brawny man. And her heart longed to know him more intimately. Resisting his affections was becoming more and more difficult. Her father's determination that she wed with Thind was breaking her heart.

She stared out the window. The sun was dimming into dusk. Reuben would be walking home from the blacksmith's soon. She gathered her skirts and shimmied out the window. A giggle escaped her lips, as she scurried over two streets to Main and pressed against the side of the Mercantile, hoping no one would see her.

Reuben walked down the boardwalk, toward his parent's house. "Reuben," she whispered.

He turned, spotted her, and cut into the space between buildings. "Wha—?" He took her hands. "What are you doing here? Your father—"

"I don't care anymore." She inhaled his musky, manly aroma that was uniquely him. "Father's not being fair."

"Maybe not, but you said—"

"I know what I said. Reuben." She swallowed. Dare she say this? Once these words were released between them, there would be no going back. A sigh escaped her, and she plunged forward. "I love you! I do not love Thind. I haven't laid eyes on him since we were so very young. Our betrothal was based on different circumstances. We are in America now, and I have no idea what happened to him or his family. As far as I know they have not corresponded with Father at all."

"Karena." Reuben captured her gaze, taking her hand and placing them against his heart. She could feel the tautness of his broad chest. A thrill shot through her.

"What are you saying?" His eyes darted between

hers.

This was it. This was the proverbial leap of faith! Here goes nothing… "Let's elope!"

Reuben staggered back. "Elope? We can't."

"Why not?" She closed her eyes. No, no, no. Was he rejecting her? Had she read him all wrong? "I love you. You love me. My Father will never change his mind about this stupid agreement of marriage he arranged for me, unless he has to. And if we are married, then, he will have to accept you, us."

Reuben searched her eyes. "Karena. I *do* love you, with all my heart. I *do* want to marry you, but we can't elope. My mother is named Honor, and we sons of Honor cannot betray that legacy. We… we have standards by which we were raised. I-we must do the honorable thing and get your father's permission. There has to be a way to convince him."

"You don't know my father. He's stubborn as a mule! He'll never change his mind." Tears rolled down her cheeks.

Reuben rubbed them away with his thumbs and kissed her lips sweetly. "We have to find a way."

Her eyes darted back and forth between his. She loved the golden flecks among the brown streaks in his eyes, the one dark spot in the white of his left eye. Had he been injured as a boy? His enviable long dark lashes that every girl would give her eyetooth to have. She sniffed. "I don't see how."

"I don't know either, but I couldn't live with myself if I didn't try."

"And… that is why I love you so much, Reuben Featherstone." She threw her arms around his neck and kissed him soundly.

He rubbed his hand up and down her back as he kissed her, then pulled away from her. He looked strained. Like pulling back from their kiss had been the hardest thing he'd ever done. They both heaved for breath. He smiled. "You better get home before they realize you are gone."

She nodded, reluctantly. He kissed her cheek and let her go. She forced herself to turn and scurry back to her window where she slipped through and went straight to her washbowl. She washed her face and combed her hair. Her lips could still feel the heat of his. Opening a tiny jar of rouge, she dabbed her little finger in the paste and touched it to her lips, to disguise their swollen appearance. Mum and Father wouldn't know, but she knew. If she closed her eyes and drew in a breath, she could still smell his manly musk and feel his arms around her.

Dinner wafted through the house. "Please, Saint Nicholas Myra," she crossed herself. "Show Reuben the way to convince my father that we belong together."

She gathered a rosary into her hands and prayed over each bead.

"Karena!" Her mother called. "Dinner."

She crossed herself, put the rosary away, and hurried to the dinner table.

"Hey, Jacob!" Reuben entered his parent's home. It was late and a plate had been left on the stove for him. He walked past it, searching for the younger of the twins. Scanning the parlor, but not finding him, Reuben rushed upstairs, striding straight to the twins' bedroom. Jacob sat at his desk, next to his bed, reading. No surprise there. "Hey, Jacob." Reuben tapped on his open door.

"Yeah." Jacob turned around, blinking.

"I need to figure something out." Reuben entered the room.

"All right. What is it?"

Reuben sat on Jacob's bed. "I need to know about arranged marriages in India and how to supersede an antiquated decision without blatant disrespect for the families."

"Whoa! Reuben, that's a lot to figure out in one night." Jacob closed his book. "I don't have a book about India or their customs, but maybe Purity or Faith can order one for the library."

"I just… need to know… what to do." Reuben hung his head and stared at his clasped hands.

"You are really sweet on this gal, aren't you? What is it… Karena? Isn't that her name?"

"Yes. And she's sweet on me, too, but she's bound by this agreement even though she hasn't seen the feller in twelve years. She…" Reuben dropped his eyes to the floor and shoved the toe of his boot into an imaginary obstacle. "She asked me to elope with her, but Jacob, you know I can't do that. It would be wrong, and Momma would kill me. I can't do it to Karena's father. He'd probably never speak to her again if we did such a disrespectful thing. I don't want to alienate her from her own parents. I just cannot do that to her."

Jacob walked to Reuben and touched his brother's shoulder. "I understand. It's not easy being a son of Honor." Jacob chuckled. "What do you want me to do?"

Reuben focused on him, gritting his teeth to keep the emotion from quivering on his lip. "I want to know if there's a way for Karena to be my wife."

Jacob stared at Reuben a long moment. "All right." Jacob jerked a nod. "I'll see what I can find."

Reuben released the breath he had been holding. "Thank you."

"Sure." Jacob patted his shoulder. "Did you eat your supper? Momma left you some on the stove."

"Yeah, I saw it. No, I came straight up here. I'll go eat now."

"Good. 'Cause if you don't eat, it won't be that girl's dad you gotta worry about offending, it'll be our momma."

They laughed and Reuben headed down to his lovingly saved supper. Could Jacob find a way? As much of a bookworm as he was, and if there *was* a way, surely Jacob could figure it out.

CHAPTER FOUR

Anushka smiled as her husband pulled their buggy to the hitching post at the only church in Lantern. The young man that had helped them every chance he could hurried to them. She glanced at Darsheel to see him frown. Anushka rather enjoyed the young man's gentlemanly gestures of kindness, and she appreciated his sensibility. He hadn't been rude or aggressive, but it was obvious he had taken a liking to their daughter and was not going to give up on winning her heart anytime soon.

Would it be wrong? They were no longer in India. America had been their chance for a new life. Was it right to tie Karena to the old ways? With the exception of here in Lantern, Texas, it had been challenging to find acceptance among those who had established the lands. People were different in Lantern and Anushka felt like they had finally found the place where they belonged. Old ways and old commitments were so distant to her heart. Did they still exist? Darsheel thought so. In fact, he clung to the idea that his honor was at stake and Karena's marriage arrangement was the thread that held his integrity intact.

It had been three years since Karena had passed the age when her marriage should have taken place. They had lost track of the Singh family when they separated in Vancouver. Darsheel wrote to their last known address occasionally, to give them a means for contact, but their returning correspondence had been silence. How could Darsheel honor such a commitment if they had no contact from the Singh family? Karena was not getting any younger. At twenty-two years of age, she deserved to marry, and if her heart's desire found someone other than Thind Singh, couldn't they, as her parents, give her permission to pursue that desire. Should the Singhs later attempt to lay claim to Karena, couldn't Darsheel accept the burden on himself for allowing their daughter to marry another because the Singhs had not made their whereabouts known to them?

Darsheel rolled his eyes. "That boy's gonna be the death of me." He spoke under his breath, but she heard him, and knew he did not have the same doubts Anushka had about their daughter and the marriage agreement made so long ago.

"Now Darsheel. That boy is very kind. Just like the rest of the people in Lantern. Look how they welcome us to their church even though we are catholic." She smiled at the approaching young man. "And look how happy Karena is when the boy comes to greet her."

The young man ran right up to their buggy and put out his hand to Anushka. She accepted his help and stepped down. Karena stepped down next. Her smile was radiant and made Anushka's heart glad. If only she could convince her husband this was right for their daughter. She waited for her husband to walk around the buggy, then took his arm.

They watched their daughter walk ahead of them with the young man. He respectfully did not take her hand but walked beside her toward the church entrance. *Reuben.* Anushka recalled his name. *Like in the Bible. The eldest son of the twelve who were chosen to lead the nations of Israel.*

Anushka smiled as she and her husband followed their daughter to the pretty whitewashed chapel on the hill. Unlike Reuben of the Bible, Anushka knew this Reuben was not the oldest of his brothers. If she remembered correctly, he was fifth of six.

His mother was a doctor and her name was Honor. How interesting these people were, and how intriguing it would be to know how they named their children. She looked forward to getting to know everyone better. There was a women's group who met regularly, perhaps she would inquire after service to see how she could join them. If she could join them. An old feeling of fear tightened in her tummy. Surely, they would be as friendly as the rest of Lantern had been and allow her to join the group. If for no other reason than to learn more about the *Indian woman* who moved to town? Surely, they were as curious about Anushka as she was about them. Most women were anxious to learn all they could about a newcomer. Why would these women be any different?

"Darsheel!" A man's voice called to her husband. His voice seemed familiar. Who in Lantern knew her husband well enough to call to him by his given name? Most everyone in Lantern referred to each other formally, Mister Khan was all she'd ever heard her husband called. Who could this be? Anushka turned with furrowed brow. "Oh, no." She whispered to herself.

Bhagat Singh and a handsome, younger version of himself walked toward the church from town. Could that be Thind? Anushka swallowed hard. Where was Anna, Bhagat's wife? When had they arrived in Lantern? How did they know she and her husband would be attending church?

"Karena!" Darsheel barked. "Come." He turned to the Singhs with open arms. "My friends!"

Karena turned from Reuben with worry in her face. Darsheel seldom spoke so harshly toward her. Anushka kept her gaze on her daughter. Confusion drew Karena's brow as she followed her father toward the two men. Then Anushka saw her daughter's realization of who these men were and why she had been called away from Reuben. Disappointment and utter sadness washed over her otherwise happy disposition. It broke Anushka's heart to see such sadness in her daughter's eyes.

Anushka wanted to run to her and take her into her arms. But she could not. Looping her arm into Karena's, Anushka walked her daughter toward the Singhs. Reuben astutely remained where he had been when Darsheel called Karena to him. That boy was very smart and knew his manners. She appreciated him not making this into a big ordeal right here outside of church service. Anushka turned her attention to the Singhs and plastered on a smile. She, too, knew the appropriate manners to display.

Introductions were in order… and questions. Lots of questions.

Reuben did not extend his elbow to Karena as they walked away from the buggy. That would have been too familiar, but he walked beside her, prepared to steady her should she stumble on the incline to the church. Being at her side felt so comfortable, and yet his nerves were on pins and needles. What to say? He had so many questions: Do you enjoy reading? Would you like to go on a picnic? What's your favorite color? Have you forgiven me for turning down your idea of eloping? How can I convince you father to call off your engagement?

He turned with Karena when her father called her name so abruptly. Reuben had never heard Mr. Khan speak so sharply to his daughter. He almost sounded alarmed, as if something of imminent danger was about to strike her. Was he angry that she was walking with Reuben? Did he find out she asked Reuben to elope with her?

Reuben knew he was pushing the boundaries of appropriate decorum, walking with a woman who was engaged to another. But that *another* was not here, nor had he been. She'd had no correspondence since they went separate ways in Canada. For all they knew, he might have died or married someone else. Why else would this other man not contact her as soon as they were of marrying age? He'd had three years to make his wishes known if he wanted to follow through with this agreement between their families.

Two men approached the Khans. Dark skinned and finely dressed, they resembled the Khans. Were they related? One looked older, the other younger, maybe the same age as Reuben. Father and son—?

"Oh, no!" Reuben's stomach fell to his ankles like a white-hot cinder dropped from his tongs. Could this be Karena's betrothed and his father?

She stiffened at Reuben's side, but obediently walked away to join her parents. Reuben's heart sank deeper into a dark oblivion with each step she took away from him. He did not walk with her. He knew he was not welcome. If this was who he suspected, he definitely was not welcome to accompany her and be introduced. She belonged to another and he had come to claim her as his bride.

People rushed past Reuben, hurrying to get inside before services started. No one wanted to be late. Uncle Harrison was known to teasingly make a spectacle of a latecomer, especially if they were one of his nieces or nephews. Once when Adam slid into church late, Uncle Harrison clasped his hand and shouted, "Praise God, we have a testimony to be shared!" And made Adam come to the front and give his testimony of redemption. It was funny when it wasn't yourself. No one wanted to give Uncle Harrison any reason to call them out for a witnessing.

Reuben stood stoic as the people bumped into his side. He could not take his eyes off Karena. His world crumbled before his eyes as the Khans greeted these visitors. Karena shied back from the younger man. If this was her fiancé, she had not seen him since she was a child. How familiar would she be with him? He didn't look like he was overjoyed seeing her, either. The twelve years that had separated them broke whatever bond they might have had as children.

Reuben could only hope.

But that wasn't fair or right. He loved Karena with all his heart and if this other man could make her happy, then Reuben would accept it. For her sake. Yet, he could not take his eyes off them. The older man wore a strained look upon his face. Khan was, well, Khan never appeared to be excessively cheerful. Mrs. Khan, too, looked strained. Like a peasant meeting a king for the first time, uncertain what to do, how to stand, or whether to stand at all. It was painful to watch. Yet Reuben couldn't turn away.

"Reuben!" Benjamin, with Jewell Ledbetter on his elbow, walked up to him. "You coming to church?"

Reuben tore his eyes off the sad spectacle and forced himself to look at his baby brother. "Sure. I'm coming." He walked with them into church. But his heart remained in the yard with Karena. Would they come to service? Or go somewhere to discuss Karena and Thind's wedding? The thought made Reuben's stomach turn over. Suddenly a sour stomach threatened his composure and he stumbled into the closest empty pew. Benjamin and Jewell sat with the rest of his family. Reuben was better at the back, alone, where he could run out if he couldn't get this feeling under control.

Service went by in a blur. Reuben didn't absorb a word. He stood when people stood, and sat when they sat, but he longed to leave. He had looked forward to today's service, possibly sitting beside Karena while Uncle Harrison preached. Inviting her parents to Momma's house for dinner after church. His mother had already agreed to having company. Little by little getting to know the Khans, and they getting to know his family.

Jacob had done the research that Reuben asked for. There was a remote possibility of winning their approval, Jacob had told him. "Without getting into the legalities about it," Reuben recalled what Jacob had found out. "If two families agree to join their children in marriage, it is binding, unless the two families later agree not to marry their children. It's all a matter of communication. Now if either party has paid the other a portion or whole dowry, then that needed to be reimbursed, goat for goat, coin for coin. Unless the two families agree to leave things as they are for having broken the promise. Nothing was said about accruing interest. And," Jacob had added. "I suppose it depends on the circumstances in which the families want to break the agreement."

Jacob's findings gave Reuben hope.

If the Khan's owed a dowry and the other family insisted on being compensated, Reuben had already decided he would ask to pay it. It would be his offering for Karena's hand. Whatever the Khans needed to validate Reuben's love for Karena and give their blessings, he would do, or find a way to do.

But he never counted on the other family coming to Lantern.

CHAPTER FIVE

The days dragged into weeks. Reuben worked hard at the blacksmith's shop. Keeping busy all day was so much better than drinking at the saloon. Suppressing his heartache was paramount. Once he got home, the pain danced in his face. Momma and his soon-to-be sisters-in-law were all a-chatter, planning the double wedding. It even seemed Benjamin had found true love in the Ledbetter gal. Another second cousin might be joining the Featherstone family. If little Ben could figure out how to keep the girl happy. Seemed those two sparked each other's tempers faster than sulfur and phosphorus.

Reuben was happy for his brothers, of course. It was just that their happiness drove his misery deeper like a dagger into his heart. Every night he dreaded leaving work. Avoiding the route home that took him by the Khan's house and resisting walking through those swinging doors where libations silenced the anguish in his heart. Life had become a challenge and accepting that Karena could not be his wife had become an impossible taskmaster.

August arrived with scorching heat and tornados

that threatened everything that was not nailed down good and solid. The blacksmith shop was busier than ever, making thousands of nails and metalworks to repair what nature swept away. Reuben felt like a tornado had swept away his heart. Numbness replaced heartache. Getting through the day became routine. Even as the double wedding approached, he knew he'd stand with his twin brothers, but he wouldn't feel anything. He just couldn't afford to allow his heart to open up to any feelings, good or bad. It was the calmest and quietest he'd ever been in his life.

The family noticed. They gave him odd, curious, and concerned looks, but no one asked him about it. There was no need. It was obvious he was not all right. Why ask? Time heals all wounds. That's what people say. Reuben doubted time would fix his broken heart. The only thing time could do was increase his numbness.

The Khans had been invited to the twins' wedding as Reuben had requested. Only problem was, he wouldn't be looking for opportunities to speak to Karena or sneak in a dance with her. He'd do his best to avoid her and the man she would soon probably marry. If Reuben thought he could get away with it, he'd skip the wedding all together. But that wasn't the honorable thing to do to his brothers or his family. No, he'd be there. At least physically, he'd be present. He couldn't promise his mind would be in attendance— or his heart.

"Oh, Thind," Karena's heart ached when Thind shared his news. They had taken a picnic out to a meadow near the Brazos River. Mum chaperoned. "I'm so sorry to hear your mother died. Where is she buried?"

"In California, where we were living before Father insisted we come here. He is adamant our marriage will honor her wishes, but—"

"But, what?" Karena stepped closer to him. "Thind, what are you not telling me?"

"Nothing." Thind turned away from her and walked toward the river. Anushka remained a short distance away. Chaperoning them from the buggy. She practiced knitting, a craft she was learning from the Lantern women's social group who met at church every Tuesday for tea and gift making.

They knitted, quilted, and sewed various items to give to the less fortunate or new brides. Would

Karena be receiving some hand embroidered tea-towels or crocheted hot pads? Her mother wouldn't say if the women were making anything for Karena's impending bridal shower. She prayed there wouldn't be a shower. It would be impossible to look happy for a solid two hours while opening hand-made gifts for a marriage she dreaded with all her heart.

The woods were full of animal sounds and bugs. It would have been romantic, should have been romantic, but it was not. Thind and she had come out here like courting couples do, but unlike a courting couple they were not consumed with bridling a blazing passion between them. In fact, Karena felt nothing but compassion for Thind. He seemed so sad. His mother had died a year ago, but there was something else suppressing his emotions. They had been friends, as children. Now they were strangers. Karena's heart belonged to another, and, if she didn't know better, so did his.

"Thind, please be honest with me. Do you want to marry me?"

His eyes shot up to meet hers. His lips pressed together, and a slight tremble rippled across them. "Of course. Our families vowed our union when we were babes. I would never disgrace your family or my own."

"That's not what I asked you." Karena touched his arm. "Thind, we were once friends, you can tell me the truth. *Please* tell me the truth."

He pulled away and walked further down the embankment. Scooping up a rock, he tossed it toward the surface of the water. It skipped five times and sunk with a final splash. Karena slowly approached him. Why wouldn't he tell her what was wrong?

Karena came alongside him. She bent to pick up a rock and tossed it in the river, also. "It's been twelve years since I last saw you. I understand if your heart… if you have found another."

He turned to face her. "Karena, I know what you are asking me." He rubbed the nape of his neck. "Why do you press me for an answer? Have *you*…" he cocked his head to one side and squinted at her. "…found another?"

Karena gazed deep into his eyes. Could she trust him to hear the truth? Or would he slap her if she admitted her love for Reuben? If they were in India, she could not admit such infidelity, but things were so different here in America. Was it different for her and Thind? "It's been so long since I last saw you.

Why didn't you or your father answer my father's correspondence? He wrote to you to let you know where we were, each time we stopped in a new town, but we never received anything from you. Did your father receive my father's correspondence? I was worried something had happened to you or you had changed your mind… about marrying me."

"Father has not changed his mind." Thind stared at the ground.

Karena opened her mouth, then shut it. Dare she speak so boldly? "Thind, that's not what I asked you. May I tell you what I think?"

He lifted sad eyes to hers. Kindness and compassion shone within his dark brown orbs. "Of course. Karena, you can always tell me what you think."

She nodded. "I think you are in love with another… in California. But your father, like my father, is set in the old ways and does not want to break the vow for our two families to merge with our marriage. But Thind, I think neither of us feel the old ways are our ways now that we are in America. We… I think we have both found our hearts' true love and wish that we could convince our fathers to release us from the obligation."

He stared at her a long moment. "Karena. *If* that were true, would it break your heart?"

"Actually, no. I am kind of hoping that *is* true for you… because… it is true for me." She sighed. That was the hardest thing she'd ever said to anyone.

He drew in a deep breath and let it out. "You are very astute, Karena. What you have said is the truth. But—"

Karena smiled. "How do we convince our fathers?"

He nodded. "Exactly."

Karena pursed her lips. "Perhaps my mother can help."

Thind looked across the meadow at Karena's mother. She concentrated with her tongue protruding from between her lips and holding the knitting needles close to her eyes. The yarn appeared to be wrapped loosely around her wrist and lost beyond her lap. A length of knitted material hung down from the activity of her working needles, but it didn't look even or uniform. "She could discuss it with your father?"

"I overheard them speaking about it the other day. While mother didn't oppose father directly, I believe if we share with her our true feelings, she would try to help."

Thind swung his gaze to Karena. "I do not mean to dishonor you, Karena. I love you… you hold a special place in my heart and my memories. But—"

"I understand. I love you. You are a dear friend to me also. But we are not *in love* with each other."

Thind took her hands into his and held her gaze. "Karena, you amaze me. I had no idea this visit would be so… amicable. Do you really think your mother can help us?"

"I told you. She has already voiced her opinion that our marriage agreement is antiquated and… she's not a fool. She knows there is someone special here in Lantern who my heart has chosen."

Thind smiled. "Tell me about him."

Karena ducked her head. The heat of embarrassment filled her face. "He is the blacksmith's apprentice and the fifth son of six. His mother's name is Honor and he seriously lives to represent her name. They all do. It's a beautiful family. His name is Reuben." She looked into Thind's eyes. "Tell me about your true love."

Thind's face transformed into joy. His smile radiated in his eyes. "Her name is Christine. Whenever I am near her… my heart leaps into a gallop that cannot be halted. She makes me feel like I could soar like an eagle if I just tried."

Karena grinned. "Yeah. I know exactly what you mean." She took his elbow. "Let's go talk to Mum."

CHAPTER SIX

"I will not hear of it!" Darsheel turned from Anushka and marched out of their bedroom. She sighed heavily. The Featherstone double wedding was in a few hours. She had broached the subject of their daughter once again with her husband while they were getting dressed. He stubbornly refused to budge from his stance that to break their vow to marry their daughter to Bhagat Singh's son would crush the integrity of the Khan family. Watching her daughter respectfully accept Thind's visitations, knowing she did not love him, and he did not love her, was slowly breaking Anushka's heart. The kids had confided in her that Thind, too, had a love interest back in California whom he wished to marry, and had asked Anushka to help convince Darsheel and Bhagat to release them from the agreement.

This was going to be harder than she thought. Darsheel could not let go of his pride in the matter. It was going to take something greater than herself to convince her stubborn husband to let these two follow their hearts. She considered whether Bhagat would be more malleable. Perhaps she could be so bold as to speak to him on their children's behalf.

Would he listen? Surely, he had been in America long enough to shed the former ways of life. As a woman, she had to tread lightly until she knew for sure what Bhagat's thoughts were.

Anushka finished dressing for the wedding and joined her husband in the parlor. Bhagat and Thind brought a large carriage rented from the Coffey Livery. The two families had agreed to go to the wedding together so that the Khan family could introduce the Singh family to the people of Lantern. Karena came into the parlor just after Anushka and dutifully stood near Thind. She looked lovely in her Sunday gown. Thind and she exchanged a smile, but they both looked sad. Anushka sighed. She had to find a way to make Darsheel and Bhagat understand this wasn't the right match.

At the church, Darsheel stood with Bhagat, introducing him to the residents as they entered the church. Karena and Thind sat with Anushka in a pew near the rear of the sanctuary, keeping space for the two fathers to sit with them. Reuben had graciously greeted Karena and Thind and then joined his twin brothers at the front where a wrought-iron arch had been decorated with flowers, greenery, ribbons, and netting. Two kneeling altars were also covered in netting and ribbon. It was a lovely set up for two brides to become wives to the twin brothers.

Mrs. Lantern softly played lovely tunes at the piano while the people of Lantern entered and found seating. Soon the music changed, and two young ladies walked slowly down the aisle. Anushka assumed they were friends of the brides. Then the music changed again to attention-getting staccato notes followed by a wedding march. Everyone stood and turned to watch the two brides who floated elegantly, arm in arm toward the front. Anushka had heard about this. Both girl's biological fathers had died in the American Civil War and they decided to walk each other down. It was so different from the India-style wedding, but lovely just the same.

Anushka dabbed at tears she couldn't help but shed. Her own daughter deserved this same happiness that glowed on these two brides' faces. Even though the Khan and Singh families sat toward the back of the sanctuary, Anushka noticed Reuben Featherstone's constant glances toward her daughter. Karena smiled and ducked her head a few times. Thind sat stoically beside her, seemingly unaware of Reuben's interest in his fiancée. Or… Anushka considered… he had no jealousy toward their flirtatious glances, because his heart belonged to another. This truly would not do. Her daughter deserved to be loved fully, not out of duty or obligation. Anushka pursed her lips. She had to convince these two fathers that their children were not right for each other.

Anushka leaned toward Bhagat. "Look at the depth of their love."

He turned to her with furrowed brow. "Beg pardon?"

"Those two couples up there. Look at how deeply they are in love."

Bhagat turned to peer at the couples each holding hands and gazing into each other's eyes. They were speaking promises as prompted by the preacher. Now that Anushka had pointed it out, Bhagat gave a half smile. "Yes. These Americans marry for their emotional attachment rather than familial alliances."

Anushka paused a moment. "Is it so bad to make such commitments based on the heart's choice?"

"For the Americans, I suppose it is not such a bad thing."

Anushka nodded to herself. A chink in his armor. There was a slight possibility she could help the children get relief from this ancient tradition.

The weddings concluded and the two couples were each pronounced Man and Wife. They ran down the aisle, grinning like the crazy-in-love fools that they were, and the people all stood to leave the sanctuary. A community dinner was set up on the church lawn, and one of the brides changed out of her pretty dress. She came back in a traveling gown. Were they leaving town that night? Anushka had heard one of the twins was moving to Boston, Massachusetts to attend Harvard Medical College. She assumed by the bride's change in clothing they would be leaving on the east bound train that came through this evening.

While Reuben kept a polite distance from Anushka's daughter and Thind, he subtly maintained a constant vigilance on her. If that girl were to stumble and fall, Anushka had no doubt, Reuben would be at her side to catch her before Thind even realized she'd tripped. No fault of Thind's, he dutifully remained near Karena, speaking to the people who greeted him, but it was obvious… so very obvious… who was in love with Karena and who was here because it was expected of him.

As the sun traversed the sky, the couples ate dinner, cut and ate wedding cake, toasted and were toasted by those who wished them well, and at last, separated. One twin brother took his bride to the Lantern Hotel for their honeymoon, and the other took his bride to the train station. The wedding attendees followed the latter to say goodbye at the depot. A wagon had been decorated with old shoes and tin cans for their ride across town. The bed held two large trunks. This *was* their move to Boston, rather than a honeymoon retreat. Other Featherstone brothers off-loaded the trunks and porters for the train stacked them along with other luggage to be loaded once the train arrived in Lantern.

Anushka and Darsheel stood back from the immediate families and loved ones, watching as what seemed like the entire town hugged and kissed the couple. More trunks were stacked next to the others as more people registered to board the east bound train. Karena and Thind, Anushka and Darsheel, and Bhagat waited patiently for the departure.

A man hollered, a horse whinnied. It pulled a small wagon but reared up on its hind legs as if frightened by something. A man swung a long whip, cracking it over the horse's backside. The horse landed and ran wildly toward the crowd of people, grazing the stack of trunks, and broke free of the harnesses that held him to the wagon. The wagon ran aimlessly into the trunks and the horse charged across the railroad tracks. The trunks toppled, coming down right where Anushka and Karena stood.

Reuben leapt out of nowhere and blocked the towering trunks from crashing onto Anushka and Karena's heads. Thind realized what was happening, pushed Karena away and grabbed Anushka's arm to pulled her further away from the avalanche of large cases. Darsheel stared at the entire chain of events that almost hurt Anushka and his daughter, then awoke from the shocked stupor and rushed to them.

"Are you all right?" Darsheel yelled.

"Yes." Anushka turned to see if Karena was all right. She seemed shaken up but unharmed. Reuben was at her side, examining her arms and shoulders to be sure she had not been hurt by the falling trunks. He looked at Anushka, running his eyes over her for signs of injury.

Doctor Honor O'Mallory, Reuben's mother, rushed up to them. She touched Karena and then Anushka as if to be certain they had not been injured. "Are you injured? Do you feel any pain?"

"Frightened, yes. Injured, no." Anushka assured the woman doctor.

Darsheel, Bhagat, and Thind approached Reuben. Darsheel shook his hand. "If it were not for your keen attention, my wife and daughter would have been severely hurt. Thank you."

Anushka smiled. She knew it would take something greater than herself to convince her husband and Bhagat that Reuben Featherstone was an honorable man. Was this incident enough to convince Darsheel and Bhagat?

Thind waited for the fathers to step away from Reuben, then he approached him, extending his hand as if to thank him with a handshake. Embarrassed by all the accolades, Reuben took his proffered hand. Thind pulled him in close, stern and serious, leaning near Reuben's ear. "Can we talk?"

CHAPTER SEVEN

Reuben paused. *Talk?* What could Thind Singh want to talk to him about? Reuben halted the handshake. The gesture of thank you was lost by the request. Reuben simply nodded. A train whistle blew west of town. Porters scrambled to organize the fallen trunks and luggage. The people of Lantern gathered alongside the platform. Their attention now on the bride and groom's departure. Reuben glanced at his brother and new sister-in-law. He needed to say goodbye.

"Give me just a minute." Reuben skipped sideways a step and pressed through the crowd to get to Jacob and Charley. "Listen, you two." He shook his brother's hand. "I wish you the best in Boston. Come back to us when you are officially a doctor." He turned to Charley and hugged her. "Write often and let us know how you're doing. You will be sorely missed."

Tears filled Charley's eyes. She smiled and nodded. Words were obviously tangled in an emotional swallow. Reuben stepped back as others took their turn to wish them well. He scanned over the heads to find Thind who waited in the clearing beyond the throng of people. Reuben worked his way out of the multitude and approached Thind. "Let's go somewhere where we can speak in private."

Thind nodded.

Reuben led him over to Main Street and down the boardwalk. The Blacksmith's shop was quiet, and no one would interfere with their conversation. Reuben had a key to get in, and Mr. O'Brien wouldn't be there. It was the logical place to take the fiancé of the woman he loved to discuss their predicament. Thind followed in silence, but when Reuben glanced his way, he appeared to be deep in thought.

How was this going to go? Would Thind tell Reuben to back off? That ruffled Reuben's feathers a bit. If Reuben had not been focused on Karena, she and her mother would have been seriously injured when those trunks fell.

Or was he seeking Reuben's thoughts on convincing the fathers to release Karena and him from this marriage agreement? After all, Reuben had made it obvious he cared for Karena so much he would put his life between her and falling trunks. He hoped Thind's intentions were for the latter. But he couldn't be sure until they were able to talk. He was fully prepared ether way. He had built up some strength swinging the smithy's hammer over the last year, he could handle Thind should he choose to start a fist fight.

Reuben jammed the skeleton key into the lock and swung the doors open wide. A lingering smell of charcoal, sizzling water, and hot metal filled the shop. He inhaled as he stepped over the threshold and waved Thind in. "We won't be disturbed in here."

"Is this where you work?" Thind looked over the tools hung neatly on the wall, the fire pit and the charcoal box. He picked up a horseshoe and examined it closely. Holding the shoe out, he turned to Reuben. "This your work?"

Reuben let a half grin curl on his mouth. "Yeah. Patrick O'Brien owns the place, but he has let me apprentice with him this past year. I'm getting the idea and don't do so bad."

Thind continued to look over the finished ironwork leaned against another wall, ready for customers to retrieve. "Looks like you've learned the art well."

"You ever beat out any metal?"

Thind jerked his head up and looked at Reuben.

"Only simple stuff like for a wagon wheel tread. Once, out of dire necessity, I reshaped a horseshoe. But nothing like this." He gestured to an ironwork gate.

Reuben nodded and crossed his arms over his chest. "So, what do you have in mind about Karena and this—"

"Look, I love Karena." Thind interrupted.

Reuben uncrossed his arms, his eyebrows shot up on his forehead, and his hands went down by his side in clinched fists. So, it was going to be a fist fight. He drew in a breath in an effort to remain calm.

"But not like you think." Thind hurriedly finished his thought. "She and I were best friends, like a brother and sister, until her father took her away from Vancouver. We rather clung to each other, terrified when we left India. The ship was huge to our small eyes, and we were all the other had for a playmate as we crossed the ocean. Her mum and my mum didn't take well to the ocean. They were sick most of the time. Rena and I were on our own in that vast boat."

Reuben relaxed his hands and listened.

Thind continued. "Vancouver was crowded and busy and… loud. We were not welcome because we were from India even though where we came from was under British rule, just like Canada. It was scary to us as small children. We were spit on and thrown out of mercantiles as if we were common thieves."

Compassion filled Reuben's chest. He swallowed but remained silent.

"When we celebrated my tenth birthday, Darsheel announced they were going to look for work in America. Of course, he suggested we come too, but my father stubbornly stayed in Vancouver, determined to make a life for Mum and me in Canada. He had a background in weaving and had brought his loom from India. But we were so severely rejected by the Canadians that we ended up working for a crew on a railway construction headed south. We lived in a tent. My Father had woven several pieces of heavy canvas which he fashioned into tents for us and the workers. Mum sewed heavy britches for the workers and cooked for the camp. Father and I both worked on the crew and when we completed the work, we stayed where the rails ended in Southern California, working odd jobs to stay alive. Mum died a year ago, and Father suddenly became determined to see that the marriage agreement with the Khans was fulfilled. To be honest, I think he is hoping this marriage will restore his financial integrity." Thind sighed.

Reuben nodded. "Karena tells me you have a gal in California that you would rather marry."

Thind grinned. "Christine. Yes. But—"

"But your father won't break his vow to Mister Khan." Reuben finished for him.

"Right."

"How do we convince these two that it is not such a disgrace in America to allow marriages of the heart?" Reuben glanced at the street through the open doors. The town was empty. The train whistle blew and faded. The train with Jacob and Charley was leaving. A sad, empty sensation pressed on Reuben's heart. He turned back to Thind. "My brother, the one who just got married and left on that train, did some research on the issue, and he tells me it's a matter of communication between the two families. If both families can agree to break the agreement, it can be broken without disgracing either family. He also said, if a dowry has been given, then it should be returned." Reuben swallowed. "Was a dowry given?"

Thind's eyes darted to the empty street. "I'm not sure. We were pledged when we were babies. A dowry has never been discussed."

"Well, I live with my mother and her husband. I don't have expenses. What I'm saying is, I've saved all my earnings, except for meals" —he remembered the breakfast, lunch, and dinner he ate at the hotel for an opportunity to see Karena when they first arrived — "and if you think your father would accept compensation to—"

"Well," Thind's eyes widened. "I don't know, but I do know my father is hurting financially. This town seems to be more accepting of foreigners settling in among the established residents. What if, somehow, you and I present Father with a job offer. His honor would be restored. I could go back to California and marry Christine, and you could marry Karena. I know she is very much in love with you. And I'm so happy for her." Thind paused, glancing around the blacksmith shop. "This just might work. Now, where do you think Father could land a job?"

Reuben smiled. "I have an idea."

CHAPTER EIGHT

"My darling, please rest." Darsheel held Anushka's arm until she was seated. "I will make the tea."

Anushka, Darsheel, Karena, and Bhagat had ridden in the large rented carriage to the Khan home after waving goodbye to the newlyweds at the train depot. As Anushka understood it, they wouldn't be back from Boston, Massachusetts for four or more years in order for the groom, Jacob, to complete a degree in Medicine. Anushka couldn't help but wonder, as did the other women in Lantern, if they would hold off starting a family until they returned.

The thought saddened her. There was only one sure way to guarantee such a thing, but she couldn't imagine a couple who had such love in their eyes for one another to maintain abstinence for four years. Would Jacob be able to finish his schooling if Charley did come into a family way?

So many concerns for the couple, all of which had already been discussed from every conceivable angle at the church-women's social where Anushka learned much more than just knitting.

Karena sat politely in the parlor but kept her gaze on the window that faced the street. Her mind was certainly elsewhere. It had not slipped Anushka's notice that Reuben and Thind had walked away from the depot together. What were they up to? Should Darsheel go find them? Could they be arguing over Karena? Neither of them looked angry when they left. Did Karena know what they intended to do?

Anushka tore her attention away from her daughter to speak to Bhagat and Darsheel. How often would she have them both in her parlor and receptive to what she might have to say. Darsheel had rushed to the kitchen to put on a kettle of water for tea and insisted she sit down. The accident with the horse and wagon tipping over the traveling trunks at the depot had not caused her any harm, nor Karena, but it did make a way for the two men to give Anushka attention that would not normally be given.

"What a wonderful wedding that was." She turned to Bhagat. "I've never been to a double wedding, have you."

He shook his head. "No. Can you imagine that in India. I'm not sure there are enough jewels in this small town to have two brides at once to be properly adorned for a Hindu wedding."

Anushka giggled. Even though she and Bhagat

had converted to Catholicism years ago, she didn't want to argue with Bhagat. She had a point to make. "And to watch two couples so very much in love. It made my heart flutter just knowing how happy they will be. Unlike poor Darsheel and me."

As if on cue, her husband came into the parlor with a tea tray. "What about you and me, my love"

"See…" she gestured toward Darsheel. "That shows you how we have adapted to the American ways of expressing affection. But in the beginning, we were rather terrified of each other." She giggled and took the teacup and saucer from her husband with a smile. She continued. "How wonderful it is here in Texas, ah, America for that matter, to let our children marry whoever their heart choses."

She glanced at Darsheel and Bhagat. If they looked angry, she would stop. If they looked receptive to what she said, she'd continue. They both looked neutral, although Darsheel appeared to tighten his jaw. That was good enough. With both father's listening to her, perhaps she could break this barrier between them and, hopefully, get them to admit their willingness to cease this agreement between Thind and Karena.

Bhagat lifted his eyes to Anushka as he sipped his

tea. "You are not speaking of those two couples we watched get married today, are you? You're speaking of Thind and Karena."

"Well," Anushka hesitated. She glanced at her husband. Had she overstepped her rightful bounds to express herself?

Bhagat continued. "We Singhs made this agreement with you Khans over twenty-one years ago while we were still in India. It was an act of solidarity between our two families. Since then we have traveled far and wide seeking the fortunes promised with coming to this continent. I personally," Bhagat pressed his splayed fingers into his chest. "Have barely kept my family alive. My Anna died of a fever that wiped out so many in our town. California is known for its mining adventures and get rich schemes, but those avenues are also so very dangerous. You, howev—"

Darsheel cocked his head back, almost daring Bhagat to continue.

He did. "Darsheel, you have found success and peace here in this town, Lantern, Texas."

Bhagat said the name and state as if it were a foreign word to him and he only knew it phonetically. "This marriage agreement between our children is my only hope for us to survive. It's the basis for most every marriage agreement in our homeland culture. Love and hearts choosing their mate does not insure prosperity or even survival."

Anushka sighed. Yes, that was the way of their homeland culture, but here things could be different. Darsheel had two good jobs with potential to become prosperous in ether one. Perhaps he could help Bhagat, and Thind for that matter, find a prosperous job here. It would be lovely to have another family from India living in Lantern. Thind could go fetch his true love from California and they could all settle here. She wasn't sure this would work or be a solution to Bhagat's concerns. Was it enough to persuade him to let their children marry the ones they wanted? "Darsheel, darling. Couldn't we find another way for the Singh's to have financial security, without Karena and Thind bonding in marriage?"

Darsheel stared at her. Of course, he did. She'd never spoken so boldly in all their marriage, she'd followed the traditions of a wife who follows her husband's lead and never questions him, ever. But they were not in India anymore. She had been exposed to very different marriage styles at the church's socials and the women's gatherings. Things were different here in America and since her husband had insisted on dragging her and Karena to this continent, why shouldn't she adapt to the local culture. "If Bhagat sees that there are opportunities for financial security here in Texas, wouldn't that give you two the freedom to release our children from this archaic bond and let them marry whom their hearts desire?"

She lifted one brow as she boldly lifted her chin. Darsheel's lips parted slightly as he went slack-jawed, staring at her. His eyes darted from her to Bhagat. "This country is heading for an economic depression. I just recently spoke to the bank president about cautioning the people to invest wisely while it is in a state of contracting. He offered me a part-time position as Financial Adviser which could expand to full-time. It is true, in a town such as Lantern, one could find a niche and prosper from it without losing your shirt or a limb as with mining for ore."

Bhagat tilted his head. "So, you feel that I could settle here in Lantern, Texas, and find a niche where I could make a hardy living and maintain an honorable position in your community, while at the same time, allow our children to break the agreement of marriage and find their own marriage partners?"

Darsheel glanced at Anushka. She held her breath. This was it. Say the right thing, please Darsheel, she begged in her mind.

His eyes returned to Bhagat and Darsheel stared at his friend for what seemed like too long. "I think they already have…"

Bhagat's eyes bulged, his mouth dropped open, and the teacup and saucer slid from his hand.

CHAPTER NINE

"Oh, my goodness, I'm so sorry." Bhagat leapt to his feet. Anushka rushed to the kitchen for a wet towel and hurried back to clean up the spilled tea and gather the broken china cup.

"No, it's all right." She pressed the wet towel into the rug.

"I-I did not know you knew Thind fancied an American girl back in California." Bhagat paled. "I told him it was impossible. We have an agreement, and I am a man of my word…"

"Yes, yes." Darsheel assured him. "Your integrity has never come into question. Even on this matter. You see… well, Anushka had mentioned the children had confided in her that Thind wished to marry another, but we have to be honest with you, old friend. Our daughter fancies an American fellow here in Lantern. Th-the one who saved Anushka and Karena from the falling luggage this very evening."

Bhagat's eyes went wide again. "Oh, he and Thind walked away from the depot, you suppose they realize who the other is? Did they go somewhere to talk? Things are beginning to make more sense to me now."

Singh sat hard on the divan as if exhausted. "It seems many have been making alternate plans for my son behind my back, including my son himself."

Darsheel gasped. "Well, no, we never—"

Thind and Reuben knocked on the front door and entered before anyone opened it for them. Karena leapt to her feet, she breathed heavily as if she had run a country mile. "What… are… you doing?"

Anushka rose from sopping up the spilled tea and slowly sat back in her chair clutching the wet towel in her white-knuckled hand. Thind humbly bowed before he entered the parlor where the parents and Karena were. "Father, may I speak with you?"

Bhagat's eyes roved over the Khans and returned to his son. "Yes, son. Of course."

Thind and Reuben backed into the foyer as Bhagat followed them. They stepped out on the porch in a huddle. Thind spoke first. "Father, this is Reuben Featherstone. He's one of the brothers to the twins who were married today."

Bhagat nodded. "How do you do. I'm Bhagat Singh." He shook Reuben's hand. "You are the American who wishes to steal my son's wife?"

"Father!" Thind snapped. "That's not how it is." He rubbed his hand down his face. "Look, Reuben and I have discussed this dilemma, and we have a viable solution. One that will satisfy everyone's needs and dreams."

Thind swallowed. It was obvious he didn't speak this way to his father often. Reuben could relate. Maintaining his honor throughout this mixed up ordeal had been the biggest challenge of his life. "Sir," Reuben swallowed hard. "Mister Singh, if I may. It is my understanding that the custom of arranging between two families the marriage of their children is to insure financial, and perhaps political, stability. I also understand that upon occasion a dowry is offered to ensure the sincerity of the groom requesting a woman's hand in marriage." He paused to assess Singh's willingness to hear more. So far, Singh remained on the porch, rather than storming back into the house, and he had not thrown up his hands or told Reuben to shut up. "I propose an option that combines those traditions and makes for a solution that will make everybody, I believe, happy. That is… if you agree with this idea."

Bhagat tilted his head. He looked intrigued. Good. Thind smiled. Reuben held back his show of mirth until he laid out their plan and Mister Singh accepted.

"Thind and I have discussed your situation. I understand you own a loom and have skills weaving heavy canvas material." Reuben paused.

Bhagat's brow knitted but he nodded.

"Ah, good. There are thousands of acres around here that belong to ranchers, and those ranchers hire a lot of men who ride across those thousands of acres which are covered by dense, thorny brush. If you were to retrieve your loom and begin making that canvas material into britches for those cowboys, it would be very profitable, and you'd be the first to bring these better wares to this area. I'd say it is a sure thing."

Singh remained silent but appeared to be thinking it over. Reuben pressed on. "Plus, because I am asking you to release Thind and Karena from this marriage agreement so she can marry me, I will give you a dowry of sorts for the disruption in your plans which you then could use to purchase a shop for your new canvas business. Your integrity will remain intact, as will Mister Khan's, and I too will have done the honorable thing to win Karena's hand for marriage."

Bhagat stared at Reuben but remained silent. Reuben glanced at the front door of the Khan's house. "If you are in agreement, all that remains is for you to speak to Mister Khan. I understand that a marriage agreement like this can be broken without losing respect as long as both families agree on severing the vow. Is my information correct? Will you speak to Mister Khan?"

Singh glanced at his son. "This is what you want?"

Thind nodded. "Yes, Father."

Singh turned back to Reuben. "Darsheel is a prideful man. I cannot make any promises until I speak to him."

"Yes sir." Reuben's heart sped up with hope. He bowed his head like he had seen Thind do earlier. "I understand. I will respect the decision either way."

CHAPTER TEN

A man stood behind a huge horse snapping a whip over its back, blocking other riders and buggies from traveling down Main Street. The travelers didn't seem to mind, the work was fascinating, and they all watched intently. A pulley and rope were attached to the horse's harness and a large wooden sign that read "Singhs' Ranch Clothing Company." A large sign was being hoisted to the top facade facing the street and Thind and Reuben were waiting with nails and hammers to anchor it into place.

"Epp." Reuben made the sound to indicate the sign was where it should be and the handler needed to stop the horse from walking any further. Thind and Reuben placed a nail and hammered it in with swift, determined swings. It was almost a competition to see who could set the nail with the least amount of hits. Bhagat Singh stood across the street and watched the shop's sign make the building become his new profession.

"It looks wonderful, Papa." Christine Singh stood at her father-in-law's side, watching with him. She and Thind had been married quickly in California before they loaded a wagon with their belongings which included the loom and her treadle sewing machine. She refused to travel to Texas with two men without first having the nuptials spoken.

Thind leaned over the facade and nailed the last nail, then straightened and glanced at his watch. "Hey, Reuben, you better get going!"

Reuben pulled his pocket watch out of his pants and flipped it open. "Oh, gosh! You're right!" They scrambled down a ladder and Reuben ran at a full-tilt dash to his mother's house. Benjamin greeted him as he ran through the back door.

"I wondered when you'd get home. Momma's got your suit laid out on your bed. She's been walking the floor wondering where you were. She and Poppa Monty have already left for the church."

"Really? Okay. I won't take long." Reuben panted and ran up the stairs.

Benjamin chuckled. "You better not! I've been left in charge of getting you to the church on time! I've got the buggy hooked up and ready to go!" He yelled at the empty stairs. Everyone else in Lantern were probably at the church by now. But it didn't hurt for the groom to be last to arrive. He's not supposed to see the bride anyway, and if he weren't there, he wouldn't be able to slip any peeks in.

In record time, Reuben jogged down the stairs in his Sunday best dark suit, his hair wet and combed neatly back from his face. "You look good." Benjamin rose and walked toward the back door. "Your chariot awaits m'lord."

Reuben chuckled. "Thanks Ben. Is Jewell meeting you there?"

Benjamin shrugged. "Who knows what Miss Jewell is doing. I hope so. That's all I can tell you."

Reuben slapped his baby brother on the shoulder. "You've got your hands full with that one, for sure."

"Yeah, but, you know, she's worth it."

Reuben smiled as he sat back and let his younger brother take the reins.

As they approached the hitching post beside the church, Honor and Purity motioned for him to hurry. "What's the hurry? It can't start without me?" He laughed, but Honor and Purity frowned.

"Never make a bride wait." Purity declared.

"You have a point." Reuben conceded. He rushed into the white chapel, then halted. It was full. Was everybody in Lantern and the surrounding area here for the wedding? Taking a deep breath, he walked steadily toward the front where Adam, Seth, and Jonah stood beside Uncle Harrison. Ben slipped in from the back and stood with the brothers. Reuben smiled at them and continued up the aisle to stand next to their great uncle. The brothers each stepped forward and shook his hand, then Reuben turned to wait for his bride.

Aunt Gloria played the piano while four girls walked slowly down the aisle and stood on the opposite side of the alter from the men. Then Gloria stopped and played the familiar wedding march. The music and the people all faded from Reuben's awareness as his eyes landed on Karena. She was covered from head to toe in a white-lace American wedding gown. Her beauty overwhelmed Reuben's mind and his heart. Adam pushed Reuben closer to Karena as her father placed her hand in Reuben's. They turned to face Uncle Harrison, but Reuben could not take his eyes off his bride. At last, Uncle Harrison allowed them to face each other and hold hands. He spoke, Karena repeated what he said, Uncle Harrison spoke again, Reuben repeated what he said. Adam shoved a fist into Reuben's arm. He turned to see the wedding rings in Adam's outstretched palm. Reuben took them and put one on Karena. She put the other on Reuben. Uncle Harrison spoke more and then told Reuben he could, finally, kiss his bride.

Reuben lifted her veil and smiled at her. Her beauty radiated through her smile and her brilliantly bright dark brown eyes. He leaned in close and brushed his lips against hers. She threw her arms around his neck and pulled him closer, engulfing his mouth with hers. Fire and desire shot through his body, passion unfurled, and he wanted nothing more but to pick her up and run with her in his arms to the hotel.

Laughter from the people brought him back to his mind and he fell back from her. They laughed together. He leaned in and breathed into her ear. "Karena, I love you with every fiber of my being. Let's get out of here as soon as possible."

She smiled, her white teeth contrasting the red rouge lip color. "Yes, my darling. I want to show you how deep my love is for you, too."

He held her hand up over their heads and the people cheered. Would they notice if he took his bride and left the rest of the celebration? Did he care? He was a son of Honor, but he had more important business to tend to. Showing his wife how much he loved her was more important than cutting a cake or toasting good wishes. He lowered their hands and hurried down the aisle.

Instructions had been to turn right, but he turned left and put her in the buggy Benjamin had prepared for bringing Reuben to the chapel. Reuben stuffed her skirts in around her legs and ran around to leap into the driver's seat. He slapped the reins on the horse's back and waved at the family, who stood with gaping mouths, as the horse trotted toward the Lantern Hotel. Benjamin stood with Jewell, they were holding hands and waving. Reuben smiled at him. Would he be the next and last son of Honor to marry?

THE END

Personal Note From the Author

Dear Reader,

I really hope you enjoyed Reuben's story. I found it the more difficult one to write. But now it is done, and I personally like it a lot. Karena and Reuben are a wonderful couple, and I love how they came together honorably. I hope you do, too. Now if you will excuse me, I'm off the write the final Sons of Honor, Benjamin.

About the Author

Lynn Donovan is an author, playwright, and director who spends her days chasing after her muses trying to get them to behave long enough to write their stories. The results are numerous novels, multi-author series, anthologies, dramatizations, and short stories.

Lynn is a co-host on a local AM radio show, KRLN 1400, called Write Time Radio where she and her co-host air old-time-radio dramas, narrations, excerpts and poems written by local writers, including herself.

Lynn enjoys reading and writing all kinds of fiction, paranormal, speculative, contemporary romance, and time travel. But you never know what her muses will come up with for a story, so you could see a novel under any given genre. All that can be said is keep your eyes open, because these muses are not sitting still for long!

Oops, there they go again…

You can learn more about Lynn on her blog at https://authorlynndonovan.wordpress.com, follow her on Twitter @MLynnDonovan, Facebook Author page at Books by Author Lynn Donovan at https://www.facebook.com/groups/BooksbyAuthorLynnDonovan and her website LynnDonovanAuthor.com.

Follow her on BookBub at www.bookbub.com/profile/lynn-donovan-9a8d7938-0798-44d7-b6e1-f52f55eb990d.

For more publications by Lynn Donovan go to: Amazon.com/author/ldonovan

Newsletter and a Free Gift for You

Hey! Thank you for purchasing and reading my book, Jonah, Sons of Honor Series. I'd like to give you a parting gift to show my appreciation. Sign up for my newsletter here: https://lynndonovanauthor.com/newsletter. I will send you an e-copy of a collection of short stories I wrote purely for your entertainment. I will happily send you this e-copy for FREE, if you ask. I will also add you to my NEWSLETTER list and you will receive up-to-date information on new release before anyone else.

This book will **not** be sold anywhere, at any time, I am keeping it exclusively for you, my readers, and only if you ask for it.

Thank you again, and God Bless.

~Lynn Donovan